For George and Jakey – P.M.

For Phil xx – C.J-I.

First published 2014 by Macmillan Children's Books
a division of Macmillan Publishers Limited
20 New Wharf Road, London N1 9RR
Basingstoke and Oxford
Associated companies throughout the world
www.panmacmillan.com

ISBN: 978-0-230-76036-3 (HB)
ISBN: 978-0-230-76037-0 (PB)

Text copyright © Paula Metcalf 2014
Illustrations copyright © Cally Johnson-Isaacs 2014
Moral rights asserted.

1 3 5 7 9 8 6 4 2

A CIP catalogue record for this book is available from the British Library.

Printed in China

# RABBITS DON'T LAY EGGS!

Written by
Paula Metcalf

Illustrated by
Cally Johnson-Isaacs

MACMILLAN CHILDREN'S BOOKS

Rupert the rabbit was bored with his burrow.
It was too dark and too lonely. Next door, he could
hear the happy sounds of the animals on the farm.

Baaaa!

Eey-ore!

Oink!

"That's where I want to live!" Rupert thought.
So he started to dig a tunnel.

On the farm, Dora the duck had just made a new nest.
It was perfect!

She was settling down to preen her beautiful
feathers when suddenly . . .

POP!

Rupert burst out of the ground!

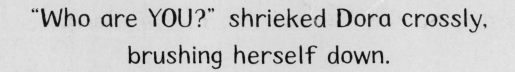

"Who are YOU?" shrieked Dora crossly,
brushing herself down.

"Hello, I'm Rupert," he said. "Can I live on your farm?"

Dora laughed. "Everyone here has a job.
Whatever could a RABBIT do?"

"I could help keep things tidy," Rupert suggested.
"I'll start with that pile of rubbish."

But Dora wasn't impressed with Rupert's tidying skills.

"That pile of rubbish was
my NEST!" she snapped.

"Oops!" muttered Rupert.

Dora sighed. Then she had an idea. "Maybe you could keep the birds away from the seeds like Scarecrow."

"I can do that!" said Rupert. And he could . . .

until he discovered how delicious the seeds were! "You're not supposed to EAT them!" shouted Dora.

Next they visited Cockerel, who showed off his magnificent call,

"COCK-A-DOODLE-DOOOOO!"

"Ooh, I can do that!" said Rupert excitedly.

He took a deep breath, threw back his head and shouted, "CROC-O-DOOGA-LOO-LOOOO!"

"How ridiculous!" laughed Cockerel. "Rabbits don't cock-a-doodle-doo."

Rupert tried again. "SOCKY-POODLE-POOOOOO!"

Dora sighed a big sigh. "Let's try something else," she said.

"What do YOU do on the farm, Dora?" asked Rupert.
"I'll show you!" she smiled.
Dora nestled down and in moments . . .

she laid a beautiful, blue egg.
"WOW!" gasped Rupert. "I wonder if I can do THAT!"

Rupert crouched down
and began to push.

But no egg appeared.
So he pushed some more.

Hrrmmph!

And finally, out popped
a small, perfectly round . . .

"Urgggh!" cried Dora, "THAT is NOT an egg!"

"You're right" said Rupert glumly. "Rabbits don't lay eggs."

"Look Rupert," said Dora, "you can sleep in the barn tonight.
But you must find a job you can do if you want to stay for good."

"Now, if you'll excuse me," she added,
"I have a nest to rebuild."

The other animals tried to cheer up Rupert with some food.
"I don't mean to be rude," said Rupert, "but why eat hay
when there's a field of delicious vegetables over there?"

"We can't get past the fence!" explained Donkey.

Rupert giggled. "Now I CAN do that!" he said. "Watch!"

And this time he was right!
He disappeared under the
fence in a cloud of soil.

Minutes later, Rupert returned, loaded with juicy carrots.
"HOOOORAY!" cheered the animals.

"Maybe Dora will let me stay now," said Rupert hopefully.

Donkey shook his head. "We can't tell her
we've eaten the farmer's vegetables!"

ZZZZZZ

They tried to think of another job for Rupert.
But their tummies were so full! And before they'd even
finished the last carrot, everyone fell fast asleep.

Soon it was morning.

"COCK-A-DOODLE-DOOOOO!"

screeched Cockerel.

But in the barn, nobody stirred.
"What a lazy bunch!" thought Dora, marching in to wake them.

Suddenly she stopped. She stared straight at Rupert.
"What is THAT?" she demanded, pointing at the carrot underneath him.

She picked it up and examined it carefully.
"Unless I'm very much mistaken," said Dora . . .

"you have LAID A CARROT! How amazing!"

All the animals giggled.
"Oh Rupert," smiled Dora, "you've found a job!"

So Rupert moved in and was very happy on the farm.
The animals were happy too, because Rupert
brought them fresh carrots every night!

Even Dora was happy . . .

especially when she discovered that carrots weren't the ONLY thing Rupert could lay!